Josie
Meets
a Jaguar

JOSIE GOES GREEN SERIES

Josie and the Fourth Grade Bike Brigade
BOOK 1

Josie Meets a Jaguar
BOOK 2

Josie
Meets
a Jaguar

by A.B.K. Bruno

Illustrated by Janet Pedersen

Dedicated to all the young protectors of the earth.

Printed in the United States.
10 9 8 7 6 5 4 3 2 1

Green Writers Press is a Vermont-based publisher whose mission
is to spread a message of hope and renewal through the words and
images we publish. Throughout we will adhere to our commitment
to preserving and protecting the natural resources of the earth.
To that end, a percentage of our proceeds will be donated to
the environmental activist group, 350.org. *We will also give a
percentage of our profits from this project directly to rainforest
conservation groups.* Green Writers Press gratefully acknowledges
support from individual donors, friends, and readers to help
support the environment and our publishing initiative.

Giving Voice to Writers Who Will Make the World a Better Place
Green Writers Press | Brattleboro, Vermont
www.greenwriterspress.com

www.josiegoesgreen.com

ISBN: 978-0997452860

Cover & book design Janet Pedersen

Additional graphics by Chelsea Silverman.
Thanks to Sonia Chajet and Will Gyurko.

Printed with soy-based inks on paper made from pulp that comes from
post-consumer waste paper in a family-owned, FSC-certified printer, lo-
cated inVermont utilizing responsible environmental, social, and economic
practices. Made with a chlorine-free process (ecf: elemental chlorine free).

FLASH!
Something shimmers
In the light
I turn around
There is a silk body standing frozen
With pride, Black holes dance forward
Glowing with glory, then it
Turns and bounds away
Poom poom poom
Tail puffing
Away behind, the silk fades
The jaguar is gone
What a sight

1

Lost

"Josie, I have to tell you something. But please don't panic."

That was my new friend Lucia talking.

"OK. No panic. What is it?"

"*Estamos perdidos.*"

My stomach dropped about a hundred miles. My brain pounded against the inside of my head. *PERDIDOS!?* LOST?!

The next thing I knew I had tripped on a root and fallen in the mud.

"Josie! Get up!" shouted Lucia.

When I got up, Lucia almost laughed.

"You have mud all over your face."

"We have bigger problems than mud," I said.

I'm not a scaredy cat. But I was far, far, far away from home. There were huge trees surrounding us, with leaves the size of an elephant's ears. Vines wrapped around the trees and drooped down all around and got us tangled. There were snakes and strange animal sounds. There was no path. It was pouring rain.

I wasn't scared.

I was terrified.

You might be wondering what I was doing lost in the Ecuadorian rainforest with a girl named Lucia. My grandma Carmen from Ecuador had set it up.

She's a marine biologist who speaks three languages and is the coolest *abuelita* in the world. She had emailed my brother Damien and me:

To: josieposie99@bearmail.com;
dgarcia43@bajo.com
From: garciacarmen86@whalemail.com
Subject: El Oriente

Queridos Damien y Josie:

If you can come to Ecuador again this Christmas, we have a chance to do something different. We can visit a family that lives in the Amazon rainforest in a village called Sayaku. It's the greenest place in the world and the family is wonderful. They even have a girl about your age, Josie, and her sister is about your age, Damien. What do you say?

Love you more than a billion gazillion infinities,
Abuelita

And we answered:

To: garciacarmen86@whalemail.com
From:josieposie99@bearmail.com
Subject: El Oriente

Querida Abuelita,

Be careful about inviting us, because we will say yes! Stand by for a special visit with us to the rainforest.

Love you back infinity times a gazillion infinities,

Damien y Josie

And now I was lost in the Amazon.
To make it worse, it was my fault.
Here's how it happened.
We had come to Sayaku a few days

earlier and Lucia and I had become great friends. I love that girl! We had gone on a picnic together, collected giant snails in the riverbed and cooked them, and went fishing in a canoe, just the two of us. We told each other all of our secrets. I even told her about my crush on Eddie, and she giggled.

So I pushed Lucia to take me on another adventure. That morning she asked her mom:

"Can Josie and I go on an adventure together?"

"What kind of adventure?

"Just walking in the forest."

"Well, OK, but go no further than the waterfall. And stay on the trail. And don't forget your lantern!"

"*Gracias, Señora!*" I said.

"*De nada,* Josie. One more thing. Lucia is the boss on this adventure and you have to listen to her."

"And when Lucia comes to Brooklyn I'll be the boss. You have to be careful in my jungle too."

Her mom laughed, "I wouldn't last a day alone in New York. But you wouldn't last a day alone in the Amazon forest."

When we started I was swinging my machete. A machete is a kind of sword used to clear a path through the jungle. It made me feel like I was an indigenous person of the forest and a great warrior. "*Yo soy de la Amazonia,*" I declared to Lucia. "*Tú eres de Nueva York,*" she answered laughing. "You're from New York." Anyway my arms got tired pretty quickly and that made me feel less fierce.

After a while I said to Lucia, "I can hear the waterfall." We stopped and listened carefully. She said, "We should follow the trail anyway." But being a big shot, I said, "We can take a shortcut by following the sound." She shook her head, but I said, "C'mon, it sounds really close." Finally, she agreed and we did a really dumb thing.

We left the trail. My fault.

We walked for a few minutes through the forest. Lucia was ahead of me and I noticed there was a small worm on her shoulder. I stopped her, but when she looked back at me she got a strange look on her face.

"*¿Qué pasa?*" I asked her. "What's wrong?"

She looked down, and so did I. There

were dozens of small leeches crawling up our boots. Some had gotten to the top of the boots and were crawling down inside them. They didn't hurt, but Ew!! They were creepy. Leeches were on the leaves, falling on us from above, and crawling up from the ground. From the look on Lucia's face, they must have been on my head, too.

"*¡Vamos!*" said Lucia. "Let's keep moving now and we'll take the leeches off later." We walked very quickly after that.

The waterfall seemed to be getting closer, because the sound was getting louder and louder. Then it started raining. Then it started pouring. Then it started pouring cats and dogs. The drops were gigantic and furious, and quickly started dripping off our hats. The sound was

a lion's roar inside my ears. It turns out, I hadn't heard a waterfall, just a tremendous rainstorm. That's why it was my fault. Oops. Big-time oops.

And that's when Lucia said, "We're lost," and I felt tears coming down my face and I slipped and fell in the mud. Plus I had to pee really bad.

"What should we do, Lucia?"

"I think I know how to get back to the trail."

"That means…"

"Yes, we have to go back through the leeches."

I must have made a horrible face. Lucia said, "If we don't want to go back there, we have to stay through the night and my family will come find us tomorrow."

With all the rain and snakes and weird
sounds, I agreed with Lucia's mom: I
wouldn't make it through a single night
alive. So we walked back through leech
land, knowing they would be falling on
us and crawling all over us trying to suck
our blood.

Suddenly I saw something different
on the tree ahead, a shape of light. At the
same time Lucia stopped and put her arm
on mine and her finger on her mouth,
calling for total silence. I stared at the
green leaves and the branches that looked
like giant snakes. I stared harder, and
then I saw it.

2
El Jaguar

El Jaguar. The Jaguar.

Lying on a branch above us, staring down at us with big yellow eyes, was a giant cat. She looked relaxed, maybe even bored. She did not take her eyes off us. I forgot about the leeches. I forgot we were lost. I forgot I was in Ecuador. I forgot I was Josie from Brooklyn. The jaguar and I just looked at each other, and it felt like forever.

Finally the jaguar moved slowly. She stood up on the branch, and then walked down it. Even though I was terrified, I noticed the patterns on her body. With each step, her shoulders moved forward and back, a little bit like the bears I'd seen in the zoo. She walked down the steep branch with no trouble at all.

Then she jumped down off the tree to the ground. She stared at us again, for what seemed like an hour but was probably less than a minute. Then she turned around and ran off through the forest, poom poom poom, disappearing in a flash. Poom poom poom.

Lucia and I hadn't spoken or even breathed this whole time. Now she said, "The jaguar will lead us to the trail." I didn't even think to ask whether that made sense. But after a little while, Lucia said "I recognize this spot."

"It doesn't look any different than anyplace to me, but you're the boss," I said. This time I meant it. A few minutes later we were on the trail again. Lucia turned on her special lantern and we headed home.

"What about the leeches, Lucia?"

"We have to take our clothes off."

"All of them?"

"Yes. The longer you leave leeches on the harder it is to get them off."

"In New York, out in the countryside, we have big ones and you have to burn them off or pour salt on them. But I never saw so many. They're on my arms, my legs, and, um, everywhere!"

Luckily these were little leeches, and

one by one we pulled them all off. Then we put our clothes back on and walked back toward the village.

"I'm glad David wasn't here," I told Lucia. "He's the brattiest kid in my school and once he ate a worm for five dollars. He might have tried to eat the leeches."

As we approached the village, Lucia's sister Leticia was walking toward us with Damien. They had been sent to look for us because we had been gone too long. They were mad. I'm not sure if they were mad because they had to come look for us or because we caught them holding hands.

3
The Shaman

All night I dreamed about the jaguar.
You know how on TV they show a great
football play in slow motion? In my
dream I had instant replay, and I watched
her walk calmly down the branch over
and over. I saw every muscle in her
body and all the black patterns on her
yellow skin. I watched her eyes watching
me. I tried to understand what she was
thinking. But she was too mysterious.

When I had watched the jaguar in my mind about one hundred times, the morning noises started. Lucia's hammock was right next to mine, so I said,

"It's still dark Luz, what's going on?"

"This is when people start cooking and stuff."

"Where is that music coming from?"

"It's my cousin's radio."

Her cousin lived next door, but the houses don't have walls so you hear everything.

Just then I heard someone clear his throat. Was that vomiting?

"Lucia! Is someone sick?" I asked.

She laughed. "No, no. My dad drinks *Guayusa*."

"Why *what*?"

"Guay-u-sa. It's a tea from a plant that grows here. A lot of grownups drink it every morning. It gives them energy. It also makes them throw up."

"Well my parents drink coffee every day and it doesn't make them puke."

Lucia's mom must have heard us talking. She said, "You can try *Guayusa* in a few years, Josie."

"No thank you," I said. "I'm good."

Lucia got out of her hammock, so I did too. We sat on one of the logs near the fire, and Lucia started painting a picture of our beautiful jaguar on the side of the lantern that had guided us home the night before. I looked at the lantern more carefully. It was a glass jar, like the ones some people keep corn or salsa in, but

Solar Powered Jar

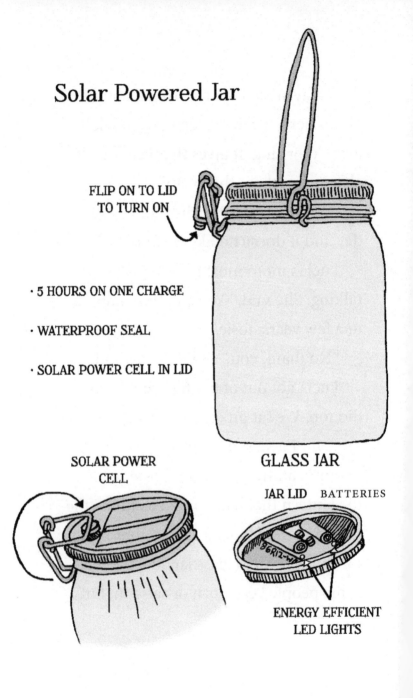

FLIP ON TO LID
TO TURN ON

· 5 HOURS ON ONE CHARGE

· WATERPROOF SEAL

· SOLAR POWER CELL IN LID

GLASS JAR

SOLAR POWER
CELL

JAR LID   BATTERIES

B6R12-W

ENERGY EFFICIENT
LED LIGHTS

the lid is special. If you leave the jar out in the sun for a few hours, it charges the batteries. Then at night when you close the jar, it lights up!

"It's gonna be a big day, right Luz?"

"For sure. When we told them about the jaguar they sent for the shaman. That's a big deal."

"What's a shaman?"

"It's kind of a combination priest and doctor. He's a very wise man who knows all kinds of things about the forest."

That afternoon all the grownups were standing in a circle.

The shaman said, "Lucia, tell us the story of the jaguar."

After Lucia told how we saw the jaguar, everyone was quiet for a minute.

Then the chief said, "Jaguars almost never come so close to the village."

One of the elders said, "The jaguar is telling us that we must pay closer attention."

Another said, "The jaguar needs a lot of room to hunt. If there's not enough forest, she will die. This might mean someone is cutting down trees in our forest."

The shaman said, "The Earth is our Mother. The forest is our supermarket. It's our drug store. Without this forest, our village will die."

Then Lucia's dad said, "The girls will lead us." We all started walking through the forest, with several men in front clearing the way with machetes. Even though they were wearing just flip flops they walked so fast I had to run to keep up. We didn't see the jaguar again, but we saw something that shocked Lucia's family even more.

4
Back in Brooklyn

"They throw up every morning?"

"Matt! I should never have told you about that. There are more important things in my story. Like saving the rainforest and the jaguars."

I was back in Brooklyn with my best friends Matt and Lizzy.

I was telling them about everything that happened in the Amazon, but all

Matt could talk about was throwing up.

Lizzy said, "You were telling us about following the jaguar."

"After we retraced our path from the day before, Lucia pointed to where the jaguar went, and we walked for about one hundred hours through the forest. Well, maybe only one hour, but it was tiring!

"And then we came to a place where there were almost no trees left, only stumps. The men starting shouting and talking a mile a minute. I couldn't tell what they were saying, but they were angry. They wanted to turn back right away. But Damien wanted to stay.

"He had done the smartest thing in his life. He brought a camera. Not a camera phone that needs electricity to charge it, but a camera with its own batteries. He asked '*¿Puedo tomar fotos?* Can I take pictures?' And here they are."

I showed my friends the photos Damien had taken.

Lizzy said, "So many trees are down."

Matt said: "It doesn't look like a place where a jaguar would go."

"I know," I said. "That's why everyone was amazed that my jaguar ran off in that direction."

"**Your** jaguar?" said Lizzy. I nodded yes. I thought of her as my jaguar.

Matt said, "There's a lot of mud. Did you fall in it?"

"Hahaha, Matt," I said.

"You know, that's deforestation," said Lizzy.

"Huh?" said Matt.

"Remember when we studied global warming?"

"Yes," Matt said. "I remember we had to learn some big words, so I stopped paying attention."

Lizzy reminded us. "Ms. Kelly said climate change—also known as global warming—is caused by electricity generation, cars, and deforestation."

Lizzy is probably the smartest kid in the class, so she *would* remember these kinds of things.

"Guys," I said. "That means this is a huge problem! The shaman said that the village needs the forest to survive. It's their supermarket and their drugstore. And the jaguar needs miles of forest to find animals to hunt. Not only that, but somehow cutting down the forest also contributes to global warming. Yikes!"

Matt said, "I know where this is going."

"Where, Matt?" I asked.

"To the library," said Lizzy. "To find out more."

Lizzy loves the library.

"Wait, before we go. I almost forgot," I told my best friends. "I brought you a present."

"I hope it's that cool jar," said Matt. "I was going to buy it from you for five dollars."

"You just saved five bucks, Matt!" I gave each of them one of the solar jars with a jaguar on it, and showed them how to use it.

5
The Library

At the library, Lizzy took down all the
books about the Amazon we could find.
We all started reading and, since you're
not allowed to talk loud in the library,
we passed notes with our favorite things
we learned.

Ecuador has three zones: Pacific Coast, Andes Mountains, and the Oriente, or Amazon Rainforest.

The Amazon is the biggest forest in the world!

Countries with some Amazon: Ecuador, Brazil, Peru, Guyana, Colombia, Bolivia, Venezuela, Suriname and French Guiana

There are a million Indians belonging to about 400 tribes in the Amazon.

The Amazon has 390 billion trees, with 16,000 different tree species. There are more than 2,000 species of mammals and bird, and 2.5 million kinds of insects!

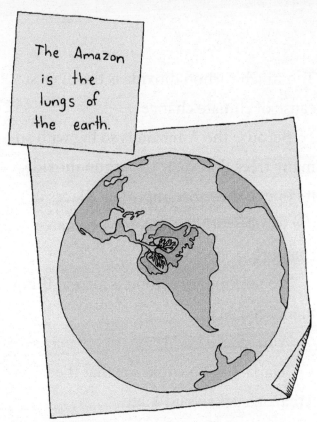

The Amazon is the lungs of the earth.

Matt's favorite factoid was, "The Amazon is the lungs of the earth," and he even drew a funny picture of it. Lizzy had been reading furiously, and she explained it like this: All the leaves in the forest inhale carbon dioxide and exhale oxygen. That's the opposite of what humans do.

Too much carbon dioxide is the biggest cause of climate change.

Because the Amazon is so big with so many trees that suck up carbon dioxide, it's one of the most important places in the whole world for stopping climate change.

"So sucking up carbon is a good thing then," said Matt.

"Um, yes," said Lizzy.

"Haha, so you could say that the Amazon sucks," said Matt.

That night I wrote to Grandma Carmen:

To: garciacarmen86@whalemail.com
From: josieposie99@bearmail.com
Subject: The Rainforest

Querida Abuelita,

Yesterday Lizzy, Matt, and I spent a lot of time studying the rainforest. We learned a ton. One thing we learned is that because people are cutting down too many trees, animals have no place to live and are dying. Some animals are even going extinct, like the dinosaurs did. That means they are gone forever! What if the rainforest had no jaguars?!

We also learned that the rainforest is disappearing at what the book called an "alarming rate." That means fast.

We have to do something.

Love you more than all the trees times billions,

Josie

P.S. I attached the pictures Damien took. He left his camera with Leticia so she can take more photos. He said he'll come get the camera next year. I think he really wants to go visit her again, if you know what I mean. ☺

6
The Photo Goes Viral

To: josieposie99@bearmail.com
From: garciacarmen@whalemail.com
Subject: Damien's photos

Querida Josie,

It is wonderful that you want to do something to protect the forests of my country.

The Sayaku people will make the decision about logging on their land. They have a very democratic system, and everyone gets a chance to help decide. Eventually they will have a big meeting and vote on whether to allow logging. If Lucia and her family want to end the logging, you can support them.

Since Damien took those interesting photos, you can start by getting them published somewhere in New York. He can write a little caption next to each one to make a story out of it.

Meanwhile, I will send printed versions down to Sayaku so they can prove what's going on. That way we'll be helping.

Love you to a zillion pieces,

Abuelita Carmen

◆　　◆　　◆

"Oh, Damien," I sang.

My brother was doodling on his bass guitar as usual. But I happened to know he needed an idea for his science project. I had heard him bragging to his friends that he was "excellent at procrastinating." That's a long word that means finding excuses not to do your homework.

"*¿Qué pasa*, Josie?"

"Need an idea for your project?"

"You know it, sister."

"How about printing the photos of logging and writing a caption next to each one."

"Hm. It would explain how the people of Sayaku live."

"Right, and how deforestation is threatening their home."

"*Buena idea. Gracias*, Josie."

"*De nada* and you're welcome, *hermano.* Besides I have to admit it was Grandma's idea."

"But you shared it with me and for that I'm going to let you help me do the project."

"Gee, thanks Damien."

His teacher loved the science project so much she sent it to the *Brooklyn Hawk*, our local newspaper. The Hawk published it online where it got thousands of views, and on Facebook everyone was liking it and friending Damien.

The BROOKLYN HAWK

Local Student Wins Photo Contest

Photo by: Damien Garcia

Then we took hard copies of the *Brooklyn Hawk* and sent them to Grandma by airmail. I had never used regular Post Office mail before. It's fun to send.

But it's even more fun to receive!

A few weeks later Matt and Lizzy were over at my house when I got an actual letter in the mail from Lucia. Not an email, not an instant message. The letter carrier who carried a big bag from house to house took an envelope out of the bag and actually put it in the mailbox.

My mom had an old-fashioned letter opener she fished out of a desk, and showed me how to use it. Lucia's letter told me the whole story of what had happened since our adventure with the jaguar.

Querida Josie,

A lot has happened since we got lost and the jaguar led us back to the path. Our chief went to the radio station in town and said that the company did not have permission for logging. The newspaper printed the photos Damien took. It got to be a big deal all over Ecuador. The head of the logging company came to our village and told us, "We are not logging in your territory." But Leticia brought out Damien's photo and the Director had to admit they were logging illegally. Then he said that if the village would agree to allow logging he would give a logging job to every man over 16 years old. So now the village is split. My dad says we are rich enough with fishing, hunting and farming. But my uncle says we need money for motors, fuel and food in case the hunting isn't good. My mom says the jaguar was sending a message that the forest is in trouble. But even my cousin is in favor of letting the company log. He works making the solar jars, but they only have a few hours of work per week. The logging company would give him work every day.

Matt interrupted: "Josie, that's it!"

"Matt, she's reading a fascinating letter, let her finish," said Lizzy.

"Okay, but I hope I don't forget."

"So don't forget."

"Forget what?"

"Matt!! Don't forget your idea."

"Oh, I don't have any idea."

"Then what were you interrupting about?"

"Lucia's idea."

"Oh, just tell us already!"

Matt said that what Lucia was saying is that if the village can make enough money making solar lanterns it won't have to do logging. It was just a matter of selling enough jars. And with a picture of our beautiful jaguar on it, everyone would want one!

The rest of the day was crazy. I called an emergency meeting of the Fourth Grade Bike Brigade and we formed a new project: Operation Solar Jar.

Edna got to work on a website with her tech genius sister.

Rafael got his Uncle Max to agree to import solar jars using his bike store company.

Jamal researched prices and figured out what Sayaku could sell their jars for in the United States.

Grandma, who joined us by video chat, agreed to leave right away for Sayaku to see if they would agree to start their own solar jar factory.

Before my friends left, Damien brought them all pizza. Damien was flying high because his photos were famous on Instagram. Also, Damien knows that pizza's important. Very important.

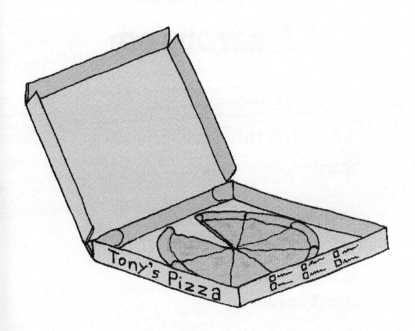

7
The Real
Amazon.com

A few weeks later Grandma emailed
again:

To: josieposie99@bearmail.com
From: garciacarmen86@whalemail.com
Subject: Solar Sayaku

Queridísima Josie,

The folks in Sayaku loved the solar jar
business idea so much that about 10

families went to town by canoe and set up a small shop to put together the jar lids. Most of the families decided that they would have at least one adult rotate in and out of town to help make the lids and ship them off.

All you have to do is send the number of orders you get, and I'm helping them set up an account to get paid directly.

I don't know if this will change the vote on logging, but this could be the start of something really big, Josie! And it was your idea!

Love you so much it's *loco*!

Grandma Carmen

Actually it was Matt's idea, though he thought it was Lucia's idea.

Anyway, here is a screenshot of the website Edna and her sister set up:

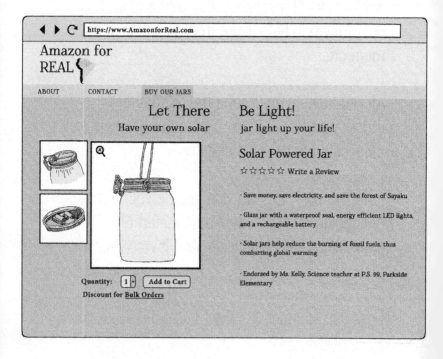

Within two weeks, we were taking dozens of orders every day for solar jars through www.amazonforreal.com

I thought about Lucia a lot. I thought she'd be happy about this.

And then, we hit a snag.

To: josieposie99@bearmail.com
From: garciacarmen86@whalemail.com
Subject: Factory too small

Querida Josie,

The strangest thing has happened.
The Sayaku Solar Jar business is *too successful.* They can't keep up with the orders, and some people are complaining about the delays and even asking for their money back.

Some people in Sayaku are saying it won't work and they'd be better off working for the logging company. The thing is they might be right, because unless we get a bigger factory, the business will fail.

We need $10,000 to buy equipment and rent the bigger space. The community doesn't have that kind of money, and neither do I.

We are still hoping for a miracle.

Love you maximum amount times all the jaguars in the world,

Grandma Carmen

I read Grandma's email to my friends.

"Whoa," said Matt. "Ten thousand dollars."

"We can do this," said Lizzy

"Aren't you listening?" asked Matt. "$10,000!"

Lizzy repeated, "We can do this!!"

"You're right." said Matt. "We have to help the people of Sayaku, who throw up every day."

Ten thousand dollars *is* a lot of money. But I'm lucky. I had the Fourth Grade Bike Brigade and Operation Solar Jar and they were ready for action.

7
The Dance

A few weeks later, it was the night of the
big fundraising dance.

When we got to the gym, wow! Edna
had been in charge of the decorations,
and boy did she do a great job. There were
streamers hanging and helium balloons
floating all around. Some of the balloons
had a drawing of a jaguar on them! She
had also made giant copies of Damien's

famous photos and put them up on the walls.

Jamal's dad runs a restaurant and brought the food. All around the gym were tables with roast chicken with rice and beans, and it smelled so great. Tony, the guy who runs the pizza place across the street from school was there, and he had boxes and boxes of pizza. That smelled really great too.

My mom had put Lizzy's hair up, so she looked very elegant. And I was wearing my special brown and red sneakers.

On one end of the gym, Damien's band was set up. The band is called Caution Tape, and they had yellow caution tape like the police use surrounding their little stage.

Rafael and his mom were taking the tickets as people came in. If they didn't already have tickets, they were selling them, and it was kind of expensive. Twenty dollars for grownups and ten dollars for kids. There was a lot of money flying around.

Ms. Blaylock took a microphone and asked for everyone's attention. She said "Welcome everyone. We are here for two reasons tonight. The first is to raise money for the Sayaku Solar Jar Company. The second is to have a good time!"

Everyone cheered.

Then she asked me to come up and explain about the Solar Jar Company.

I brought one of the jars with me and explained. "This jar catches rays from the sun. The top of the lid stores the energy in the panel. At night, if you close the lid, the metal points touch and the battery turns on the light.

"Matt, lights please." Matt turned off the lights and I turned on the lantern. Everyone could see it glowing. "OK Matt, lights back on." Nothing happened. "Matt?" But Matt didn't turn on the lights. Instead he turned on his own lantern. He had put some marbles in the bottom of the jar, behind the picture of the jaguar. The marbles lit up the jaguar and it glowed with a rainbow of colors. It looked really amazing. The crowd went *ooh* and *ahh*. Finally he turned on the lights. Leave it to Matt to bring a surprise.

Then I finished my little speech. "These solar jars are made in a little factory in Ecuador by the people of

Sayaku. They live in the rainforest, but they also have an office and a small factory in town. We know that they can sell thousands of these jars, but first they need to build a bigger factory. They have great houses, boats, fresh food, and they live in the most beautiful place. In some ways they are very rich people. But they don't have a lot of money. So that's why we need to send them about $10,000 to buy new equipment and build a bigger shop."

Then Ms. Kelly got up. She put on her most scientific teacher voice and explained, "These jars are good for the climate because they reduce the burning of fossil fuels for electricity. Burning those dirty fuels is what causes global warming. Making these jars will be a safe alternative to logging in the Amazon rainforest. Friends, these solar jars are a win, win, win! Save the jaguars!!"

All my friends started clapping and whooping.

Then Rafael's Uncle Max started an auction. He took one of Damien's photos and started talking about it and asking how much will you pay for this photo. He was talking so fast it was funny. "Who will give me $20 dollars for this amazing photo do I hear 20 yes who will give me 30–30 dollars from the man in the tie 40 do I hear 40 dollars…" People started raising their hand to bid $50 dollars and even $100 dollars for a photo. Then he auctioned a bicycle and lots of other stuff people had donated.

Soon it was time for the dance.

Damien plays bass, and his friends play piano, guitar, and drums. They play all kinds of great songs, and some of them they write themselves. After they played their first song, Damien took the microphone and said, "And now we have a surprise. Please welcome to the stage our very own Ms. Sheyla."

Ms. Sheyla came up to the stage and said, "I would like to teach you all a new dance. It's called The Jaguar."

And Ms. Sheyla busted a move! That's what Damien says when someone is a good dancer. After the drummer started playing a cumbia rhythm, she rolled her left shoulder, and then her right one, and then she walked in time to the music, lifting her knees high. She moved like a jaguar!

"C'mon, Everybody!" she said into the mic. And everyone in the gym started dancing the new dance. My whole class got into a circle, even the boys, and we were all doing The Jaguar, first in one direction, then in the other. Then we just started dancing any old way.

I looked down to see my own steps. My brown and red sneakers were moving on the gym floor. They looked good. Then I looked up again.

Eddie was dancing right next to me.

It was one of the funnest nights ever. I stayed late with Rafael and a few grownups to count up all the money we raised. It came to $12,199.86.

Would that be enough? Would Sayaku vote against logging?

8

The Wait

To: josieposie99@bearmail.com
From: garciacarmen86@whalemail.com
Subject: Sayaku Assembly

Josie, this is the last email I will send you for
a few days. Today I'm getting in the canoe to
go to Sayaku, where, as you know, there is no
internet or phone service. I'm going because
they are having a big *asamblea* – an assembly.
It's different from a 4th grade assembly

because it lasts for several days. At this asamblea, the community will decide whether to allow logging on their land or not.

As soon as I get back to town, I will call to let you know what happens.

Love you a gatrillion *pedazos*,

Abuelita Carmen

A few days can be a long time. When we were in Sayaku, there was no phone, no email, no text, and no teenagers with Whatsapp. I liked it when people paid attention to me and didn't always look down at their devices. But now I wanted Grandma to be able to text my mom or dad the second there was a decision about logging. Instead I would have to wait until she got back to town.

That was Sunday. I didn't think I could stand to wait.

So I called for Matt and Lizzy to go for a bike ride. We rode all around the park, but the whole time I kept thinking about what was happening in Sayaku. I was wondering what Lucia was doing and I guess I got careless, which is not good when you're riding a bike. Suddenly I biked into a tree and toppled over. Matt and Lizzy came running over to help me. Then they saw I was okay and started laughing their heads off.

On Monday after school, my mom took me swimming at the YMCA. After we changed into our suits, I walked straight into the glass doors and banged my nose. Then I saw Eddie on the other side of the pool. I started walking over to say hello, but I guess I didn't watch where I was going, and the next thing I knew I was in the pool. Eddie and his friends were laughing so hard they almost fell in the pool themselves.

On Tuesday Lizzy said, "Josie, you are really losing it. Riding into trees, falling into pools. Come back to planet Earth."

"I can't stand waiting to find out what they decide."

"You've done everything you can do. You got Damien's photo in the paper. You got companies to sell Sayaku Solar Jars. You raised twelve thousand dollars for the jar factory!"

"The logging company doesn't care about that stuff. They want the trees."

"Listen Josie, I need some help with *my* forest project. Would you help me?"

Of course Lizzy probably didn't need any help at all. But that's how she got my mind off waiting.

Lizzy's project was about New York City's Million Trees Program. That's the mayor's plan to plant a million trees, all just in our city.

For the next three days we studied everything about trees. Instead of rainforest trees, Lizzy's report was about forests around New York.

We learned a ton.

MILLION TREES PROJECT: BROOKLYN

🍂 There are about 600,000 trees on streets of New York City and even more than that in the parks.

🍂 Before the Europeans came there was forest almost everywhere.

🍂 In the 1800s people cut down a lot of the forest to make way for farms and cities.

ZELKOVA

5 OF THE MOST COMMON TREES IN BROOKLYN

PIN OAK

LONDON PLANE TREE

HONEY LOCUST

AMERICAN LINDEN

🍂 With a million new trees, NYC will be taking CO2 out of the air and putting in more oxygen.

🍂 The Million Trees project will make the city greener and help fight climate change.

🍂 There is more forest in New York State today than there was 100 years ago.

On Friday Lizzy was presenting her report. It was fantastic of course.

In the middle of her presentation, the loudspeaker in our room started crackling. It always crackles before an announcement. "Attention, Attention." It was the voice of our principal, Ms. Blaylock. "Josie Garcia, please come to the office right away. Repeat: Josie Garcia, please come to the office immediately."

Oh no! What had I done? This was the second time this year I had been called to the principal's office, and that is not a good thing.

Ms. Sheyla gave me a pass and everyone watched me walk out of the classroom. My knees were shaking when I walked to the office. Ms.

Blaylock was waiting for me. "Josie, I'm sorry to take you out of class. There's an emergency phone call for you. It's from Ecuador."

Emergency! Ecuador! Lizzy's presentation was so great I had almost forgotten.

I picked up the big, old-fashioned, black phone. "Hello?"

"*Hooolllllaaaaa Josie! Soy Abuelita Carmen.*"

"Hi Grandma!"

"I just got back to town from Sayaku. How are you?"

How am I? Who cares, I thought! But I didn't say that.

"Fine, Grandma. What happened at the *asamblea*?"

"I delivered the money for the factory to the chief. He sends his thanks to you and to the whole community of Parkside for its support."

Get to the point Grandma, I thought! "He is very welcome. *Abuelita,* what happened??"

"You know how it is there, Josie. Everybody in the community was there. First there was a big feast. And the next day there were long speeches. And ceremonies with drumming and singing."

"*Abuela!*"

"The logging company people came and talked about how they care about the forest, too, and they promised a lot of jobs."

"*Abuelita*, you know this is an international call, it's very expensive."

"Oh that's OK Josie, I don't mind because this is very important."

"Then please tell me!"

"Oh. Yes. Well, Sayaku decided to…" Just then the other phone rang in the office and I couldn't hear what she said. I pushed the phone hard on my ear to try to hear better.

"Could you repeat that, Grandma?"

"Weren't you listening?"

"Of course I was but the other phone rang. Oh please just tell me Grandma!"

"The Sayaku Asamblea voted to stop all logging in its territory."

This was it. This was the news I was dying to hear.

"Grandma that's fantastic, that's fabulous, that's amazing."

"Yes it is. And I'll tell you something

else. Some people say it was because of the new solar jar factory. There are enough jobs now. People can work and at the same time protect the forest."

I was so happy I couldn't speak.

"Josie I have to go now. Good work, *Hija*. I will tell you more about it soon. *Adiós*."

"*¡Adiós, Abuelita! ¡Muchas Gracias!*"

I hung up, and just then there was a big cheer. I turned around and my class was all crowded around the door to the office.

"They decided to stop the logging," I shouted.

"We know," said Ms. Sheyla. Ms. Blaylock *accidentally* left the loudspeaker on."

"Oops, I guess I did," said Ms. Blaylock, smiling.

Lizzy said, "We heard everything, Josie. *Felicidades* and congratulations!"

It was the happiest moment of my life.

We all went back to the classroom, and Ms. Sheyla put on some music. It was Damien's cumbia song. And she did The Jaguar at the front of the room. Then all the kids were doing The Jaguar and singing along to the music.

School was never like this before. And then just when I thought it couldn't get any better, Tony walked in with boxes of pizza pie.

Lizzy said "Wow, who ordered all the pizza?" Ms. Sheyla had the biggest smile on her face.

She knows that pizza's important. Very important.

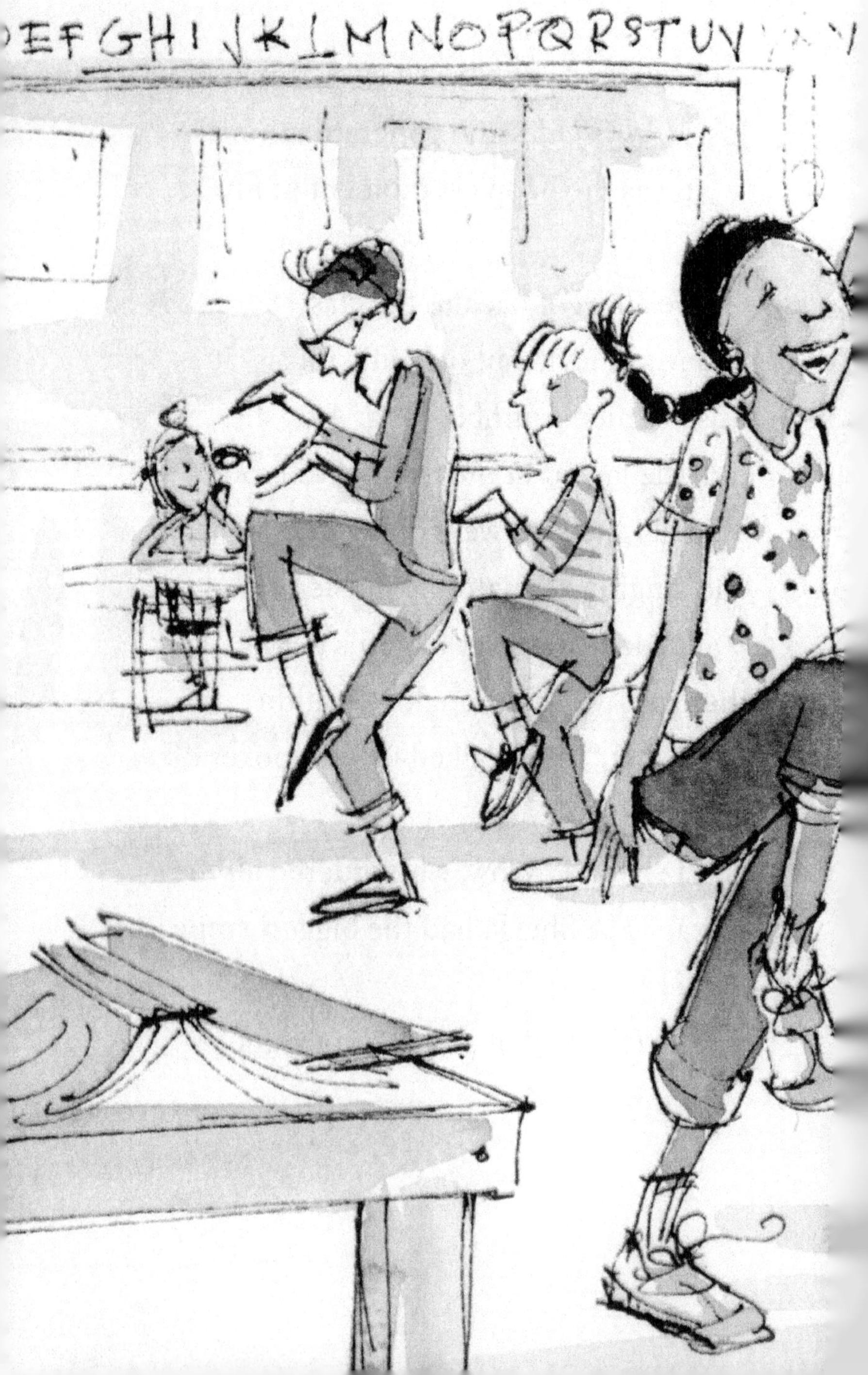
EFGHIJKLMNOPQRSTUV

About the Jaguar

The jaguar, a mystical and magical creature, has long been a symbol of power and strength to many indigenous cultures. Today, jaguars face growing danger from deforestation and development; they are literally disappearing from our planet, with only 15,000 estimated to still roam the wild. But there is hope. Their last remaining stronghold is in the Amazon basin.

The web of life on Earth depends upon biodiversity, and many animals in the Amazon depend upon the jaguar. The range and habitat requirements of a single jaguar is broad and thus when preserved, many other species are also protected. The survival of jaguars is critical to maintaining a delicate balance within the rainforest ecosystem.

As jaguars and other creatures of the Amazon are interconnected, so is our work to protect them. Our ability to thrive as a species on Earth is dependent upon the peoples, plants, and animals of the Amazon.

Josie Goes Green
Meet the Authors

Josie Meets a Jaguar is the second book in the *Josie Goes Green* series. It is co-authored by the Bruno/Handman family: Beth, Kenny, Antonia, and Benjy. The series is inspired by the enthusiasm of the students from P.S. 321, where Beth is Assistant Principal and Benjy and Antonia attended elementary school. Kenny works coordinating environmental campaigns. Benjy teaches ESL and outdoor skills for children. Antonia works for Global Alliance for Incinerator Alternatives as a grant writer and communications coordinator. Our hope is that the *Josie Goes Green Series* inspires young people to take action on climate change and to become protectors of the earth. Our family is from Brooklyn, New York.

Josie and the Fourth Grade Bike Brigade

Bill McKibben, the nation's leading author on climate change and the founder of 350.org said, "The Bike Brigade are real heroes, not only because they bike but because they organize."

Josie and the Fourth Grade Bike Brigade was the first in the *Josie Goes Green* series about Josie Garcia, a feisty nine-year-old girl from Brooklyn who becomes a crusader for preventing disastrous climate change and other environmental threats. In each book, Josie takes simple, ingenious actions that bring real changes to her neighborhood and the world. The book are for ages 7-11 and are appropriate for schools, school districts, children's social issue book clubs, and families.

Available as an audiobook on Audible as well!

Josie and the Trouble With Trash

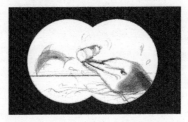

Thanks to teachers strike in New York City, Josie gets to ride the waves, swim with dolphins, and visit an island of trash in Ecuador. Back in Brooklyn, the garbage is piling up on the sidewalks, and there's just too much stuff! Josie notices something odd: some of the same trash shows up in Brooklyn and Ecuador.

The same kids who brought you the Fourth Grade Bike Brigade in Book 1 and Operation Solar Jar in Book 2 are ready to solve that mystery, and they're ready for action. Their Don't Be Fooled Committee decides to reduce waste by LOSING a contest that their principal wants to win. But just as they are making progress, Josie's brother Damien, who has been acting strangely, goes missing. And that leads to the biggest surprise yet in the *Josie Goes Green* series.

CPSIA information can be obtained
at www.ICGtesting.com
Printed in the USA
LVOW03s1211100317
526737LV00002B/2/P

9 780997 452860